Published by Hachette Partworks Ltd.
ISBN: 978-1-909766-68-6
Date of Printing: March 2019
Printed in Romania by Canale

Disney

The Fox and the Hound

Disney

Hachette

One spring morning, a mother fox and her cub were being chased by a hunter and his dogs.

When she came to a patch of tall grass, the mother put the cub down. Then she ran off, hoping the hunter would follow her and not notice her baby.

A little while later, gunshots
rang out. The cub waited and
waited for his mother, but she
didn't return.

Luckily, a kind owl called
Big Mama had seen what had
happened.

"Don't worry," she said to the
cub. "Big Mama'll find someone
to take care of you."

Big Mama went to
her friends, Dinky the
sparrow and Boomer the
woodpecker.

"The fox cub has lost his
mother," Big Mama told
them. "And Widow Tweed
lives all alone. Maybe
she could take the cub
in? I reckon she'd like a
companion!"

When the warm-hearted widow spotted the little cub in her garden, she immediately took him inside and fed him some warm, sweet milk.

"You're just like a toddler," smiled the old lady. "I'll call you Tod, for short."

Meanwhile at the next-door farm, a hunter called Amos arrived home with a brand-new puppy.

"His name is Copper," Amos told his old dog, Chief.

"This pup'll be a big help to us when he's older," said Amos. But Chief wasn't so sure!

One day, Copper went for a sniff round the
forest and came nose-to-nose with a fox cub!
Before the day was over, the pair had become
best friends. They didn't know that foxes and
hounds were supposed to be sworn enemies.

That evening when Copper
came home, Amos tied him
up so that he couldn't run
off again. Just then, Tod
appeared. He'd come to visit
his new friend.

But when Chief caught Tod's scent, he chased after the cub. Amos heard the commotion and ran outside. When he saw Tod, he thought the fox had come to steal his chickens.

Amos chased Tod back to Widow Tweed's house. "Keep that fox away from my chickens!" he yelled.

Widow Tweed was scared. She knew that Amos would shoot the fox if he saw him again.

"Tod, you'd better stay in the house for now," she said. Poor Tod missed his new friend very much!

Meanwhile, Amos was getting ready for a big hunting trip.

"Chief! Copper! Come on, we're heading for the mountains," he called. "The hunting season has started and I don't want to miss a minute of it!"

Amos and the dogs spent the whole winter in the mountains. In the valley below, Tod waited every day for his friend to return.

One day, he met Big Mama. "Be careful," she warned Tod. "You and Copper are grown up now, so you can't be friends any more. His job is to chase foxes like you."

In the spring, Amos, Chief and Copper came home. Copper, now a big, strong dog, howled along happily to Amos' singing. Chief didn't think much of their musical talent!

That night, Tod heard Copper's howl and crept
out of the house to meet his friend. But, to Tod's
surprise, Copper told him to go away.

"We can't be friends any more," Copper
explained sadly. "I've got a job to do, and that job
is to catch foxes."

Suddenly, Chief appeared and chased Tod onto a nearby railway bridge – just as a train appeared! Chief had to jump off the bridge into the water below.

Copper was furious – he thought that Tod had pushed Chief off the bridge. He promised to make Tod pay for what he had done to poor Chief.

Widow Tweed knew it
was time for Tod to live
in the wild, as he was
meant to. She took
him to a clearing
in the forest.

"This is your
home now,
Tod," she said,
hugging him.
"Be happy."
Tod sadly
watched her go.

Luckily, Big Mama turned up with someone that she wanted Tod to meet. The stranger was a pretty lady fox called Vixey. Soon Tod had a new friend!

One day, the two foxes heard gunshots. Amos and Copper were on their trail!

Just as Amos took aim at the foxes, a huge bear rushed out at him. Amos stepped back, right into a steel trap!

Copper bravely tried to protect his master, but the powerful bear swiped him away. When Tod heard Copper howling, he raced back and jumped on the bear.

Tod led the bear towards the river, away from Amos and Copper. Tod jumped onto an old tree trunk overhanging the water, but when the bear followed, the trunk gave way. Tod and the bear both plunged into the river!

The bear was swept away
by the current. Tod
managed to struggle to
the riverbank, only to
find Amos pointing a
gun right at him.

Copper couldn't let Amos hurt his friend, so he stood in Amos' way, his eyes pleading.

Amos lowered his gun. "You're right," he said to Copper. "The fox saved us from the bear."

Amos went to see Widow Tweed and told her about his adventures with the bear. She was very proud of Tod's bravery.

Tod and Vixey
walked together back
into the forest. Tod had
learned that the two
most important things
in life were friendship
and love – and he was
lucky enough to have
them both!